This book belongs to

Jacen A Price

D1421374

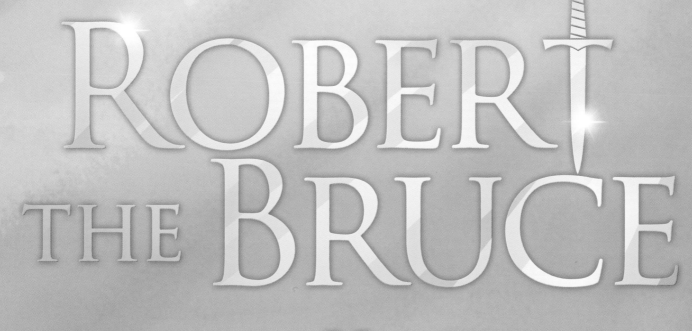

ROBERT THE BRUCE

THE KING AND THE SPIDER

ILLUSTRATIONS BY

TERESA MARTINEZ

Robert the Bruce lived 700 years ago.
He was descended from an ancient
Scottish king and was known for
his bravery.

In Robert's time, the kingdoms of Scotland
and England were at war. When the old king
of Scotland died, King Edward I of England
invaded and tried to rule Scotland too.

Robert the Bruce believed that the Scottish
people should have their own king. He battled
King Edward in support of the famous freedom
fighter William Wallace. But in 1305 Wallace
was captured and Edward had him killed.

Robert the Bruce was shocked and angry. He knew Scotland needed a leader, so he asked the country's lords to support him. In March 1306, at Scone Palace, he was crowned King of Scotland.

King Edward was furious and swore that he would conquer Scotland completely. His army fought King Robert's forces and defeated them five times. Then, finally, at the Battle of Methven, Edward attacked at night, taking the Scottish men by surprise...

King Robert looked over the battlefield at Methven. There had been a fierce but short fight, and now the English soldiers were capturing the last of his small army. The cries of the injured and imprisoned men left Robert sad at heart: the battle was lost. This was the sixth time he had been defeated.

"Ride, Sire!" urged John, his trusted steward. "If you are caught, we can never win!"

The king swung onto his horse. "I will return!" he shouted, as he galloped away.

Yet months passed and King Robert could not return. He hid, but King Edward's forces hunted him everywhere. Needing a new safe place, he set sail with John for the castle of a friend, Sir Hugh Bysset.

King Robert was heartsick. "I hate running away."

"You must escape or be killed, your majesty," replied John.

They sheltered safely for the winter. But one evening, Sir Hugh had news: "Sire, King Edward is seizing your castles and jailing your family. He will not give up until he has found you."

"How will you stop him, your majesty?" asked Sir Hugh's daughter, Brianna.

Robert looked desperate, but he didn't answer. He could no longer imagine defeating his enemies.

That night, Brianna dreamed of burning castles and fearsome soldiers. She woke in fright and looked out at the bright moon.

On the waves, the wind whipped swirls of mist into fantastic shapes: mermaids and sea serpents and selkies, and a ghost ship sailing towards shore. Brianna looked closer. No, it couldn't be…

She ran down the corridor and burst into the castle's Great Hall.
"Your majesty, an English ship is sailing towards us," she cried.
"They've come for you!" said Sir Hugh to King Robert. "To the
beach, my friend! Hide in the sea cave. My loyal men will fight them off."

"I don't know why I keep trying," Robert muttered as John rowed him to the secret cave. "Edward has beaten me six times."

"Be strong, your majesty," replied John.

The king nodded wearily. "Farewell, John. Good luck in the fight." He splashed through shallow water to the back of the cave, where he sat alone in despair.

King Robert waited through the long, dark, shivering night. Then just before dawn, in a shaft of moonlight, he noticed a spider hanging from the cave mouth on a length of silvery silk.

"This is no place for a little spider," he said sadly.

The spider tried to swing from one side of the cave mouth to the other, but missed.

"Poor wee thing," Robert murmured.

The spider needed to build a web. It swung on its slender silk again – and again missed its target.

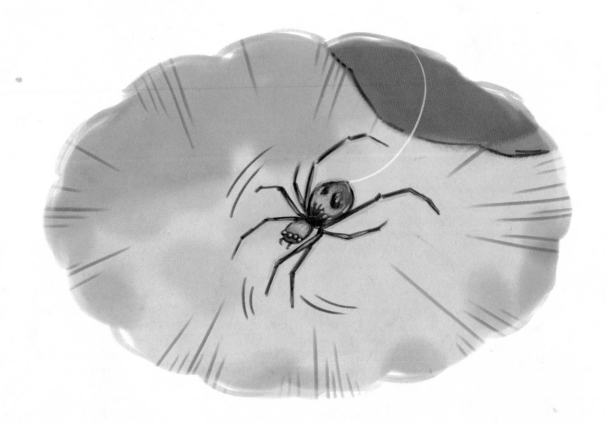

Six times it tried, and six times it missed.

But Robert did not pity the tiny creature any more; he admired it.

"Come on, wee lassie," he whispered. "You can do it!"

The spider took a mighty swing – and landed on the far side!

"Well done, wee lassie!" Robert roared in delight. "You did it!"

He stopped and wondered aloud, "Six tries, then success! I was beaten six times, but like the spider I will keep trying!"

Suddenly Robert heard a shout. It was John, in the rowboat. "Good news! Thanks to Brianna's warning, we defeated the English sailors!"

He rowed the king back to the castle to congratulate Sir Hugh and his men.

"My friends, you saved my life," said Robert.

"But Sire, Edward now knows we are here," warned John. "We must find a new hiding place."

Robert smiled. "I will hide no longer! Farewell Sir Hugh, farewell Brianna. Today I will return and I will fight once more."

King Robert and John sailed back from Sir Hugh's castle, and the king gathered a new army. His forces grew in strength until finally, at Bannockburn, close to Stirling Castle, they faced King Edward II, the son of Edward I.

As dawn broke on the battlefield, King Robert addressed his troops.

"My loyal soldiers, Edward's army is twice the size of ours. But one night I watched a small spider spin a web in a cave. Her determination inspired me. Small can be powerful! If we are determined, then, like that spider, we will surely win, and Scotland will belong to the Scots!"

His army roared.

The battle raged for two days until King Robert's brave army pushed the English troops back against the fast-flowing burn. Edward's forces were trapped, like prey in a spider's web.

"Victory!" shouted King Robert. "We were beaten, but we did not give up, and this time we have won!"

King Robert's victory over King Edward II at the Battle of Bannockburn changed Scotland's history. Robert drove out the English troops and was finally able to reign over his country.

King Edward III of England, son of Edward II, accepted King Robert as the rightful ruler of Scotland.

When he died, the body of Robert the Bruce, King of Scotland, was laid to rest at Dunfermline Abbey. He asked for his heart to be buried at Melrose Abbey — and it is still there now.

Today, Robert the Bruce is a Scottish national hero. You can
see his statue at Edinburgh Castle.
    The legend of Robert the Bruce and the spider tells us:
if at first we don't succeed, try, try again.

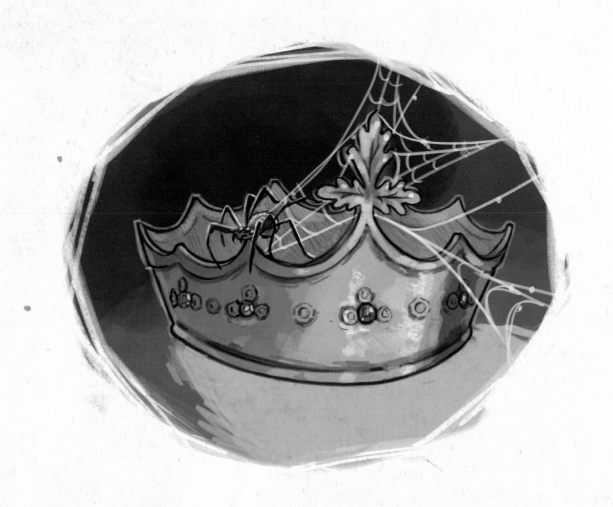

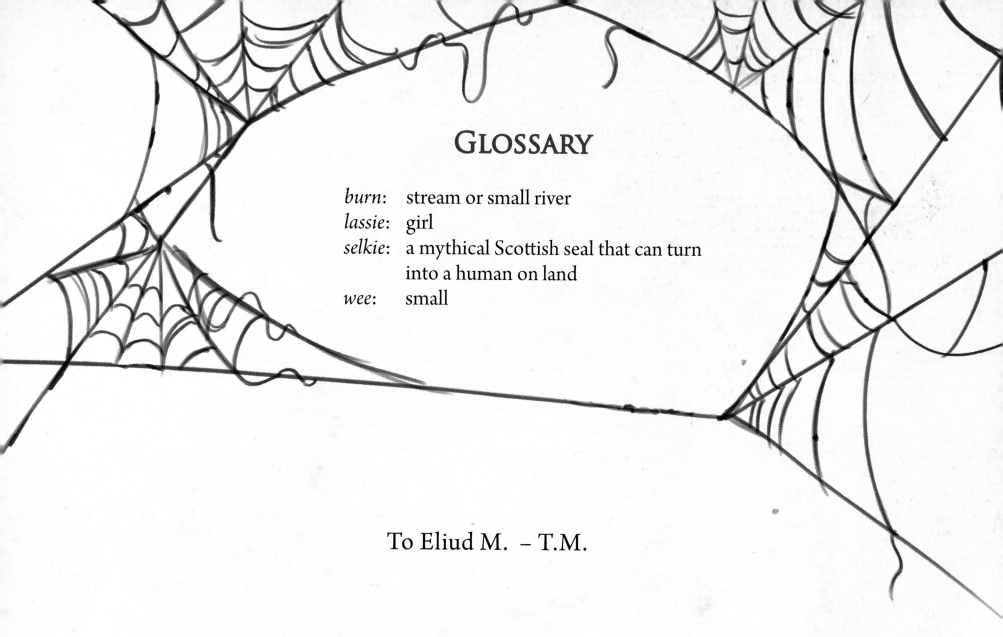

GLOSSARY

burn: stream or small river

lassie: girl

selkie: a mythical Scottish seal that can turn into a human on land

wee: small

To Eliud M. – T.M.

Kelpies is an imprint of Floris Books. First published in 2019 by Floris Books

Text © 2019 Floris Books. Illustrations © 2019 Teresa Martinez

The publisher acknowledges subsidy from Creative Scotland towards the publication of this volume

British Library CIP data available. ISBN 978-178250-558-7
Printed in Malta by Gutenberg Press Ltd